Boss

written by Pam Holden
illustrated by Kelvin Hawley

1

Bossy Bear wanted to go to sleep for the winter, but he could hear all the noises the other animals made as they played outside his cave.
"How can I ever get to sleep? I don't want to hear any more noise," he grumbled. "I must get rid of all these noisy animals."

He thought of an easy way to catch the animals that annoyed him. His idea was to build a trap that they would not see until they had fallen in. That night, Bear dug a hole and hid his trap by covering it with leaves. "Ha, ha," he chuckled to himself, "That won't be noticed until it is too late!"

Early the next morning, Goat came trotting along, trip trap, and fell through the leaves into Bear's hidden trap. "Help, help!" he bleated as loudly as he could. When Bossy Bear heard the bleating, he hurried to see what he had caught.

"You make a loud bleating noise, Goat," grizzled Bear. "I want to go to sleep for the winter, so I'll take you far away where I can't hear your noisy bleating."

4

"I'm sorry I kept you awake," said Goat. "You can take me far away, but whatever you do, please don't leave me up on the mountain."

"That's just where I will take you," growled Bear. "I'll be able to have a nice, quiet sleep when you have been left up on the mountain."

He took Goat high up on the mountain, which was just the right place for a goat to be.

6

Later that morning, poor Monkey fell through the leaves into Bear's trap. "Help, save me!" he chattered, as Bossy Bear hurried to see what he had caught. "You are only a small, chattering monkey," he growled, "but you make a loud noise. I'm trying to go to sleep for the winter. I'm going to take you somewhere so far away that I can't hear your chattering."

8

"I'm sorry," said Monkey. "Wherever you take me,
please don't put me into the deep, dark forest."
"That's exactly the place to put you," growled Bear.
"I will be able to have a long, quiet sleep when you are
in the forest."
He took Monkey to the forest, where he went swinging
away through the trees.

That afternoon, Duck waddled along and fell into
Bear's tricky trap. When Bear heard loud quacking,
he hurried to see what he had caught.
"You are only a small animal, Duck," he grizzled, "but
you make a loud quacking noise. I need to go to sleep
for the winter, so I'm going to take you far away
where I can't hear your quacking."

"I'm sorry," said Duck. "Take me far away, but please don't leave me near the pond."
"That will be a good place to leave you," growled Bear. "I'll have a nice quiet sleep when you have been put into the pond."
Bear chased Duck into the pond, where she swam happily away with her family.

13

That evening, Pig fell into the hidden trap. He grunted and squealed until Bossy Bear came to see what was in his trap.

"You are too noisy, Pig," he growled. "Your grunts and squeals keep me awake. I can't get to sleep for the winter, so I will take you far away where I can't hear your grunting noise."

"I'm sorry I kept you awake," said Pig. "You can take me far away, but whatever you do, please don't put me near any mud."
"That's a good idea," growled Bear. "I can have my winter sleep while you are stuck in the mud."
Bear pushed Pig into the mudhole, which was exactly the place Pig loved to be.

When all the animals were back in their own homes, everything was quiet. Bossy Bear settled down happily in his cave for his long winter sleep. ZZZzzzzzzzzz! As soon as the animals knew that Bear was asleep for the winter, they came back out to play, and they made as much noise as they liked.